The Cookie Thief

by

Christopher M. Sandoval

Illustrated by Daniel Gallegos

Dorrance Publishing Co
585 Alpha Drive
Suite 103
Pittsburgh, PA 15238
Visit our website at *www.dorrancebookstore.com*

ISBN: 978-1-4809-5004-7
eISBN: 978-1-4809-4981-2

The Cookie Thief

Once upon a time there was a bear named Charlie. Charlie lived all by himself in a cozy little cottage in the forest. Every afternoon, Charlie whipped up a batch of cookies. Charlie loved cookies. He always made five cookies because five seemed to be the perfect amount for a nice mid-afternoon snack.

One day, Charlie made five cookies and left the cookies to cool in the window while he took a short nap. Charlie always had his cookie snack after nap time. While Charlie slept the forest was filled with the delicious smell of fresh-baked cookies.

On this particular day, a little bird named Willie smelled the delicious aroma. Like Charlie, Willie lived all alone in the forest and he loved cookies.

"What a wonderful smell," Willie thought to himself. Without really thinking, Willie couldn't help but follow the delicious

DGallegos

scent. Before long, Willie arrived at the window where Charlie had left the cookies to cool.

Willie flew onto the plate and took a long loving sniff.

"Mmm, chocolate chip, my favorite!" Willie peaked inside the cottage to see if anyone was watching. Nobody seemed to be home. The cottage was very quiet. The longer Willie stayed the harder it was to resist tasting a cookie. Finally, Willie decided to take a tiny taste.

"Mmm, this is the most fabulous cookie I've ever eaten." Before long

Willie had eaten one whole cookie. Willie sat back against the window frame and rubbed his stuffed little tummy (you see, it does not take much to fill a little bird like Willie).

A little while later, Charlie awoke from his afternoon nap and was anticipating a delicious cookie snack. However, as Charlie approached the window the anticipation on his face was replaced by a puzzled stare.

"Hmm, that's funny," said Charlie. "I was sure I baked five cookies, but I only see four cookies here on my plate. Oh

well, I suppose I'll just have to eat four cookies for my cookie snack today." Even with one less cookie, Charlie's cookie snack was as good as ever.

The next day, Charlie baked five cookies and took his afternoon nap as always. And again, when he woke from his nap he only found four cookies. This pattern continued for several days. By this time, Charlie suspected that there was a cookie thief nearby.

The next afternoon, Charlie baked five cookies as always. However, this time Charlie did not take a nap. Instead, he hid

DGallegos

behind a large rocking chair and waited. Charlie waited for what seemed to be a very long time. Finally, a little bird flew down to where the cookies were cooling.

"Maybe that's the cookie thief," Charlie whispered softly. Just then, Willie took a cookie in hand and began eating. Willie was enjoying the afternoon treat so much that he didn't notice the angry bear that was stalking close behind. Suddenly, right in the middle of a delicious morsel, Willie found himself in the tight grip of a very large and stern-looking bear.

DGallegos

"So you're the cookie thief!" Charlie shouted in an angry voice. Willie was still too shocked and frightened to answer. "Tell me, my little thief, how were they? You would certainly be qualified to critique my recipes."

Willie finally answered in a shaky voice, "W-W-Why mister bear sir, you're cookies are the most scrumptious I've ever eaten."

Charlie felt very pleased. "Yes, they are rather yummy," Charlie said proudly. Willie shook his head in agreement. "Over the years, I've made them all several times. Peanut butter, oatmeal, chocolate chip, oatmeal raisin, and so on and so on. Tell me, my little thief, what was your favorite?"

"Oh, I fancied them all, mister bear, sir," replied Willie.

"But you know, thief," Charlie continued. "I've become rather bored eating only cookies for my snack. I was just thinking that a roasted little bird would be a nice change of pace. What do you think?"

A great wave of fear came over Willie like nothing he had ever experienced before. “Oh, please spare me, mister bear, sir!” Willie said in desperation.

“Why should I?” Charlie retorted.

“I will be forever in your debt, mister bear, sir.” Charlie’s grip tightened for a moment. The little bird closed his eyes half expecting to be gobbled up at any moment.

“Well, you can start by never coming here and eating my cookies again!” Charlie said as he angrily threw the little bird out the window. Willie, his heart still beating like a drum, quickly flew away feeling ashamed and very lucky to be alive.

2017

The next day, Charlie baked five cookies and took his afternoon nap while the cookies cooled. During his nap, Charlie began to dream about the time when he was a young bear cub and had stolen tomatoes from Miss Chicken's vegetable garden. Miss Chicken had severely scolded him that day and he woke from his nap trembling. This time, all five cookies were left on the plate. With plate in hand, Charlie settled into a comfortable chair and ate his cookie snack.

For several days, Charlie baked five cookies and there were always five cookies left after his nap. Gradually, Charlie began to feel a little guilty about the way he treated Willie.

"Perhaps I was too hard on the little fellow," Charlie said sadly. "Besides, it was nice to have company for a while, even if he did steal some cookies." As the days went by, Charlie missed Willie more and more. Furthermore, the cookies just didn't seem to taste as good as before.

One afternoon, when eating his cookie snack, Charlie had a wonderful idea. "That's it!" Charlie said with a big grin. "Besides, the little fellow owes me one."

The next day, Charlie baked six cookies and set out to find Willie. Finally, after a long search through the woods, Charlie found Willie sitting under a tree and nibbling an apple. "Well, hello there, my little thief," Charlie said warmly.

"Hello, mister bear, sir," Willie returned. The little bird no longer feared the bear because his words were spoken in a tone of sincere kindness.

"Wonderful day, wouldn't you say?"

"Why yes, it's a beautiful day," Willie replied.

Charlie reached down and gently cupped the tiny bird in his massive paw. "You know I was just thinking how wonderful it would be to have someone share my cookie snack with me. Would you be interested?"

At hearing this, Willie's face lit up like a little child on Christmas morning. Willie wrapped his tiny arms around the large bear's neck in a loving embrace. "Why yes, yes, I would love to share a cookie snack with you!" Willie said as tears of joy welled in his eyes.

That afternoon and for several afternoons to follow, Charlie and Willie enjoyed a cookie snack together.

"Besides," thought Charlie, "it's a lot more fun to share your cookies with a friend."

THE END

CPSIA information can be obtained
at www.ICGtesting.com
Printed in the USA
LVHW07n2254190918
590746LV00005B/15/P